W9-DBI-434

Dear Parents:

Congratulations! Your child is taking the first steps on an exciting journey. The destination? Independent reading!

STEP INTO READING® will help your child get there. The program offers five steps to reading success. Each step includes fun stories and colorful art or photographs. In addition to original fiction and books with favorite characters, there are Step into Reading Non-Fiction Readers, Phonics Readers and Boxed Sets, Sticker Readers, and Comic Readers—a complete literacy program with something to interest every child.

Learning to Read, Step by Step!

Ready to Read   Preschool–Kindergarten
• big type and easy words • rhyme and rhythm • picture clues
For children who know the alphabet and are eager to begin reading.

Reading with Help   Preschool–Grade 1
• basic vocabulary • short sentences • simple stories
For children who recognize familiar words and sound out new words with help.

Reading on Your Own   Grades 1–3
• engaging characters • easy-to-follow plots • popular topics
For children who are ready to read on their own.

Reading Paragraphs   Grades 2–3
• challenging vocabulary • short paragraphs • exciting stories
For newly independent readers who read simple sentences with confidence.

Ready for Chapters   Grades 2–4
• chapters • longer paragraphs • full-color art
For children who want to take the plunge into chapter books but still like colorful pictures.

STEP INTO READING® is designed to give every child a successful reading experience. The grade levels are only guides; children will progress through the steps at their own speed, developing confidence in their reading. The F&P Text Level on the back cover serves as another tool to help you choose the right book for your child.

Remember, a lifetime love of reading starts with a single step!

For A.M.B., keeper of dreams

Text copyright © 1984 by Harriet Ziefert. Illustrations copyright © 1984 by Norman Gorbaty, Inc. All rights reserved. Published in the United States by Random House Children's Books, a division of Penguin Random House LLC, New York.

Step into Reading, Random House, and the Random House colophon are registered trademarks of Penguin Random House LLC.

Visit us on the Web!
StepIntoReading.com
randomhousekids.com

Educators and librarians, for a variety of teaching tools, visit us at
RHTeachersLibrarians.com

Library of Congress Cataloging-in-Publication Data
Ziefert, Harriet.
Sleepy dog / by Harriet Ziefert ; illustrated by Norman Gorbaty. p. cm.
Summary: Simple text and illustrations portray a small dog getting ready for bed, sleeping, dreaming, and waking up.
ISBN 978-0-394-86877-6 (trade) — ISBN 978-0-394-96877-3 (lib. bdg.)
[1. Bedtime—Fiction. 2. Dreams—Fiction. 3. Night—Fiction. 4. Dogs—Fiction.]
I. Gorbaty, Norman, ill. II. Title. PZ7.Z487 Sl 2003 [E]—dc21 2002013650

Printed in the United States of America 92 91 90 89 88 87 86 85 84

This book has been officially leveled by using the F&P Text Level Gradient™ Leveling System.

Sleepy Dog

by Harriet Ziefert
illustrated by Norman Gorbaty

Random House New York

Chapter 1: Sleepy Dog

"Time for bed, sleepyhead."

Sleepy, sleepy,
up to bed.

Head on pillow.

Nose under covers.

Cat on bed.

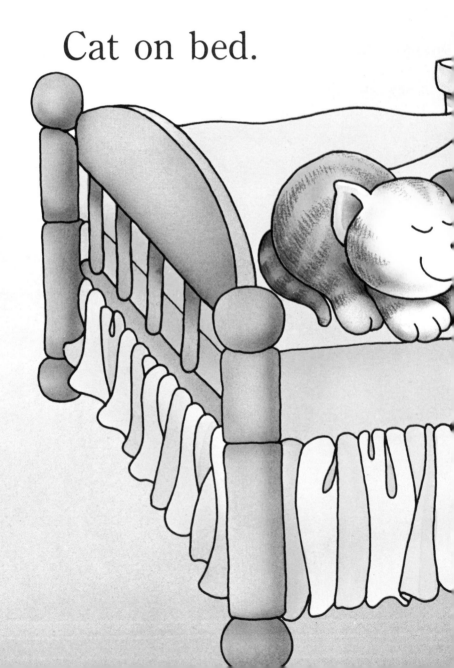

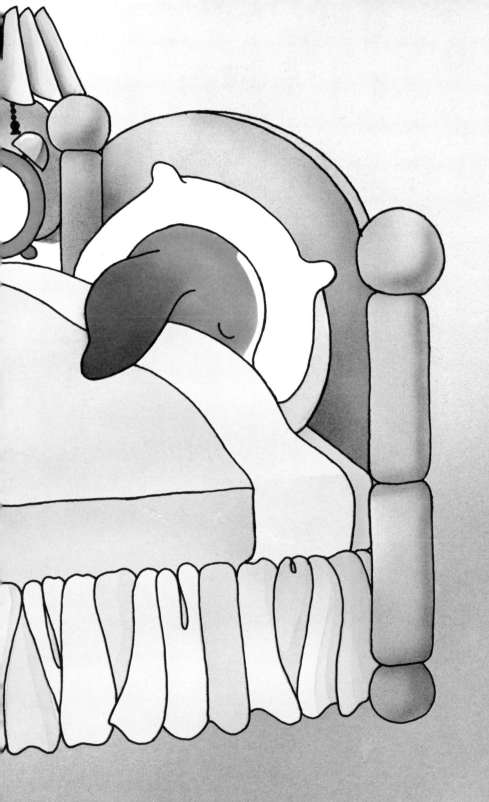

Kiss me.

Kiss me good.

Kiss me good night.

Turn on the moon.

Turn off the light.

Sleepy, sleepy,
sweet dreams tonight.

Chapter 2: Dreaming

I dream

I am eating.

I dream

I am jumping.

I dream

I am running.

Someone is
chasing me.
HELP!

Now I am awake.

I need a drink
of water.

Sleepy, sleepy,
back to bed.

Chapter 3: The Clock

Tick, tick, tick, tick.
The clock says
tick, tick, tick, tick.

The clock shouts
ring, ring, ring!
Wake up!

Turn off the moon.

Turn off the clock.

Turn on the sun.

Turn on the light.

Good morning, cat...

time to play!

"Good morning,
little dog."